Cookie Angel

Bethany Roberts 🐎 Illustrated by Vladimir Vagin

HENRY HOLT AND COMPANY ❄ NEW YORK

Henry Holt and Company, LLC
Publishers since 1866
175 Fifth Avenue
New York, New York 10010
www.henryholtchildrensbooks.com

Henry Holt® is a registered trademark of Henry Holt and Company, LLC.
Text copyright © 2007 by Barbara Beverage
Illustrations copyright © 2007 by Vladimir Vagin
All rights reserved. Distributed in Canada by H. B. Fenn and Company Ltd.

Library of Congress Cataloging-in-Publication Data
Roberts, Bethany.
Cookie Angel / by Bethany Roberts; illustrated by Vladimir Vagin.—1st ed.
p.   cm.
Summary: On Christmas Eve, the Carroll family goes to sleep after making a special
angel-shaped cookie, which then comes to life and must quickly learn to act like a real angel
when some of the toys misbehave and threaten to ruin Christmas.
ISBN-13: 978-0-8050-6974-7 / ISBN-10: 0-8050-6974-7
[1. Angels—Fiction. 2. Toys—Fiction. 3. Christmas—Fiction. 4. Cookies—Fiction.
5. Singing—Fiction.] I. Vagin, Vladimir Vasil'evich, ill. II. Title.
PZ7.R5396Coo 2007   [E]—dc22   2006030070

First Edition—2007 / Designed by Laurent Linn
Printed in the United States of America on acid-free paper. ∞

10 9 8 7 6 5 4 3 2

To my own Christmas angels:
Bob, Krista, and Melissa

—B. R.

It was Christmas Eve.

Santa's magical snowflakes fell softly outside the Carroll home, whispering Christmas secrets.

Inside, snug and warm, the Carrolls were busy baking Christmas cookies. They mixed and rolled and cut and baked.

The very last cookie they made was an angel. They gave her yellow frosting hair, a pink frosting dress, and a big candy O for a mouth.

"She needs sprinkles on her dress," said Holly.

So they added sugar sprinkles.

"She needs a songbook," said Christopher. "All angels sing."

So Mr. Carroll, humming a Christmas tune, added a songbook with blue icing.

"She's beautiful!" said Holly.

"The prettiest cookie we've ever made," said Mr. Carroll.

"We will hang her on the tree," promised Mrs. Carroll. "But now it's time for bed. Christmas morning will be here soon!"

The children were tucked into bed and kissed good night.

"Sweet dreams!" said Mr. Carroll.

"Good night, my darlings," said Mrs. Carroll.

Soon the children were fast asleep.

Mr. and Mrs. Carroll hung the angel on top of the tree.

In the moonlight, Cookie Angel's sugar dress sparkled like tiny stars.

"I can almost hear her sing!" mused Mrs. Carroll on their way to bed.

"Anything can happen on the night before Christmas," *whispered the snow.*

Soon the house was still. The only sounds were the whispering snow, the ticking of the grandfather clock, and Old Sherlock, the family dog, snoring in the corner.

Until . . . the grandfather clock struck twelve.
BONG, BONG, BONG, BONG, BONG, BONG,
BONG, BONG, BONG, BONG, BONG, BONG!

"Now!" whispered the snow.

Cookie Angel blinked her eyes and began to sing. *"Hark! the herald angels si-ing! Glory to . . .* Bless my candy buttons," she said. "I can sing!"

"What's an angel?" asked T. Bear, who was sitting under the Christmas tree.

"I'm an angel," said Cookie Angel. "But I don't know much about it. I just got baked."

"Did you come with an instruction book?" asked T. Bear.

"I have a songbook," said Cookie Angel.

Cookie Angel quickly flipped through her songbook. "Let's see," she said. "Real angels sing . . . a lot!" Cookie Angel flung her arms open wide. She sang a snatch of this, a snatch of that, getting louder with each song.

> *The first Noel, the angels did say . . .*
> *. . . Sing, choirs of angels . . .*
> *. . . Angels we have heard on high . . .*

"Are real angels this loud?" asked T. Bear.

Just then there was a commotion under the tree.

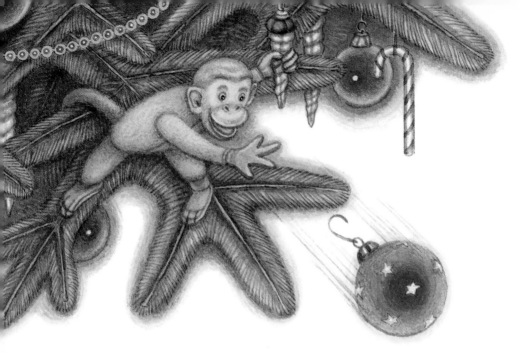

A plush monkey, swinging from bough to bough, was throwing glass balls to the floor.

CRASH!

CRASH!

"Oh, dear," said Cookie Angel, peering down at the floor.

"What a mess!"

"Chi, chi, chi!" Monkey giggled. He grabbed a candy cane from a tree branch and threw that to the floor, too.

The candy cane landed right on Jack-in-the-Box.

"I want a candy cane, too!" cried Doll.

Jack-in-the-Box jumped up and down. "Mine, mine, mine!"

Doll and Jack-in-the-Box tugged on the candy cane. It snapped into pieces.

"WAAAAH!" cried Doll.

"This will never do," said Cookie Angel. Suddenly her wings
fluttered. "Holy popcorn balls!" she said. "I can fly!"

With a flap,

    and a flip,

      and a flop,

she landed—PLOP!—right on top of T. Bear.

"Oof!" said T. Bear. "Are real angels this clumsy?"

As she landed, a cookie shoe broke off. "Pleased to meet you,"
said Cookie Angel, wriggling her bare toes.

"Are you my mama?" asked Doll.

"No, I'm Cookie Angel."

"WAAH," cried Doll. "I want my mama!"

Jack-in-the-Box rolled his eyes. "I wish I had a *boy* to play with."

Rocking Horse neighed. "Nothing is going right around here!"

Cookie Angel pulled down two candy canes. "One for each of you," she told Jack-in-the-Box and Doll.

"Monkey is ripping open the presents!" shrieked Doll.

"No, no, Monkey," said Cookie Angel. "Those presents are for the children!"

Cookie Angel marched in front of the toys. "What we need to do," she said, "is sing. Music makes everything better."

Doll sniffed and wiped her eyes. T. Bear picked up a tambourine. Jack-in-the-Box found a trumpet under a doll carriage.

Cookie Angel tied some jingle bells around Rocking Horse's neck, and Monkey found a drum.

"The angels in my songbook all have gold harps. But this will have to do," she said, sitting down at a tiny piano. "All together, now. Ready? Sing!"

> *Deck the halls with boughs of holly.*
> *Fa la la la la, la la la la!*
> *'Tis the season to be jolly.*
> *Fa la la la la, la la la la!*

Cookie Angel plinked. T. Bear rattled. Rocking Horse jingled. Monkey banged. And Jack-in-the-Box blew on the trumpet. TROOOOT!

With all the clatter, the family dog, Old Sherlock, roused from his sleep. He padded over to Cookie Angel and sniffed. "Woof?"

Then with a big, wet tongue, he took a lick of her sugar dress.

"Help!" cried Cookie Angel.

T. Bear snatched her up and put her on top of a table. Then he bopped Sherlock on the nose with his soft paw.

"Ooooow!" It was just enough to send Old Sherlock shuffling back to his corner by the fireplace.

"Are you okay, Cookie Angel?" asked T. Bear.

"Yes," said Cookie Angel. "But that monster licked the sugar sparkles off my dress." She looked at her dress forlornly.

"Neigh!" said Rocking Horse. "So what else could go wrong tonight?"

Just then, Monkey, in a shiny red racing car, screeched around the corner.

VR-ROOM! VR-OOM!

"Chi, chi, chi!" Monkey giggled.

"He's heading into the children's room," wailed Doll.

"He'll wake the children and spoil Christmas!" cried Cookie Angel.

"Stop him!" shouted T. Bear.

ZOOM!

The toys dashed into the children's room after Monkey. Cookie Angel flew as fast as her tiny wings would carry her.

In the excitement, Cookie Angel forgot to look where she was going. She flew into a bedpost and bent her halo. "OH! OH! OH!" she moaned.

"I'm sure real angels don't have crooked halos," said T. Bear, reaching toward Cookie Angel. "There! Now it's straight."

Just then, Old Sherlock poked his nose into the doorway.

"Oh, no," cried Cookie Angel, remembering Old Sherlock's big, wet tongue.

"Oops!" Cookie Angel teetered, then slipped from her perch on the bedpost. She somersaulted in the air three times and landed under the bed.

THUMP!

T. Bear threw himself down in front of Monkey,
but the red racer zoomed right over him.

Monkey zipped under the curtains,
flashed past a bookcase, and sped around the
dollhouse. Then, careening around a curve at top
speed, he spun out of control.

"Look out," yelled Jack-in-the-Box.

"Whoa!" said Rocking Horse.

Nestled near the children's beds was a little manger scene. Monkey was spinning straight for it!

"He's going to crash into the manger!" cried Doll.

T. Bear crawled under the bed. "You're an angel," he said. "Do something!"

"But I'm not a real angel," said Cookie Angel. "I'm just a cookie angel."

"You can sing!" said T. Bear.

Cookie Angel looked quickly through her songbook. "There must be something that will help," she muttered. "HO! This one! Ah-choo!" Cookie Angel raced from under the bed, dusty and dirty.

"Silent Night," sang Cookie Angel. "Come on, everyone, sing!"

> Silent night, holy night.
> All is calm, all is bright.
> Round yon virgin, mother and child,
> Holy infant so tender and mild.
> Sleep in heavenly pe-eace,
> Sle-ep in heavenly peace.

The peaceful sound of the toys' voices filled the night air.

"A-roo!" Old Sherlock moaned softly from his corner by the fireplace.

Monkey yawned. He rubbed his eyes.

PPPT! PPPT! PPPT! He slowed, then came to a stop, right by T. Bear's fuzzy feet.

"Peppermint praises!" said Cookie Angel.

The children stirred in their beds.

"Look," whispered Cookie Angel to Doll.

Doll peeked at the sleeping girl in the bed. "Mama!" she said softly.

Jack-in-the-Box looked at the sleeping boy. "My boy! My boy!"

Monkey beamed and jumped up and down. "Chi, chi, chi!"

"Monkey wants a boy, too," said Jack-in-the-Box.

Cookie Angel tiptoed over to the manger and stared. "Bless my candy heart!" she said. "This must be the baby in my songbook."

Rocking Horse sniffed the hay.

"The baby needs a soft place to sleep," Cookie Angel told him.

Then in her clear, high voice she began to sing. *"Away in a manger, no crib for a bed . . ."*

The manger baby opened his eyes and smiled at Cookie Angel.

Cookie Angel glowed.

"You look like a real angel now," said T. Bear.

"You're bea-u-tiful," said Doll.

BONG, BONG, BONG, BONG, BONG, BONG! The clock struck six.

"Glory to gumdrops," said Cookie Angel. "Back under the Christmas tree, all of you! Christmas morning is almost here."

"I'm going to dream about my mama," said Doll as Cookie Angel tucked a warm, cozy blanket around her in the doll carriage.

"I'm going to dream about my boy," said Jack-in-the-Box.

"Chi, chi, chi!" said Monkey, nodding his head. He curled up around his drum.

Rocking Horse rocked. His bells jingled gently.

T. Bear snuggled against a velvety pillow. Cookie Angel tied a big red bow around his neck.

She sang softly, *"Sle-ep in heavenly peace."*

"Hush, hush, hush," whispered the snow.

One by one, everyone dropped off to sleep.

"*Sle-ep in heavenly peace!*" Cookie Angel sang as she, too, drifted off to sleep.

And Santa's snowflakes whispered, "Merry Christmas!"